W9-CCO-375

AARON ZENZ

MONSTERS Go Night-Night

ABRAMS BOOKS FOR YOUNG READERS • NEW YORK

The line art in *Monsters Go Night-Night* was created with ink and brush and then digitally colored in Photoshop.

Cataloging-in-Publication Data has been applied for and may be obtained from the Library of Congress.

ISBN for hardcover edition: 978-1-4197-1653-9
ISBN for this edition: 978-1-4197-3201-0

Text and illustrations copyright © 2016 Aaron Zenz
Book design by Alyssa Nassner

Originally published in hardcover in 2016 by Abrams Appleseed, an imprint of ABRAMS. This edition published in 2018 by Abrams Books for Young Readers. All rights reserved. No portion of this book may be reproduced, stored in a retrieval system, or transmitted in any form or by any means, mechanical, electronic, photocopying, recording, or otherwise, without written permission from the publisher. Abrams Appleseed is a registered trademark of Harry N. Abrams, Inc.

Printed and bound in China
10 9 8 7 6 5 4 3 2 1

Abrams Books for Young Readers are available at special discounts when purchased in quantity for premiums and promotions as well as fundraising or educational use. Special editions can also be created to specification. For details, contact specialsales@abramsbooks.com or the address below.

ABRAMS The Art of Books
195 Broadway, New York, NY 10007
abramsbooks.com

For Elijah, the Monster-Maker

MONSTERS eat bedtime snacks.

Which snack

do **MONSTERS** eat?

MONSTERS eat UMBRELLAS!

MONSTERS
take baths.

What do **MONSTERS** take baths with?

MONSTERS
take baths with
CHOCOLATE PUDDING!

MONSTERS
wear pajamas.

What kind of pajamas do **MONSTERS** wear?

MONSTERS
wear
TOILET PAPER!

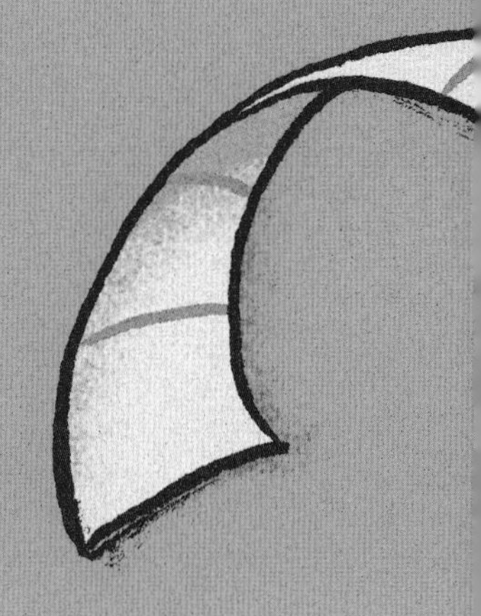

MONSTERS like to snuggle.

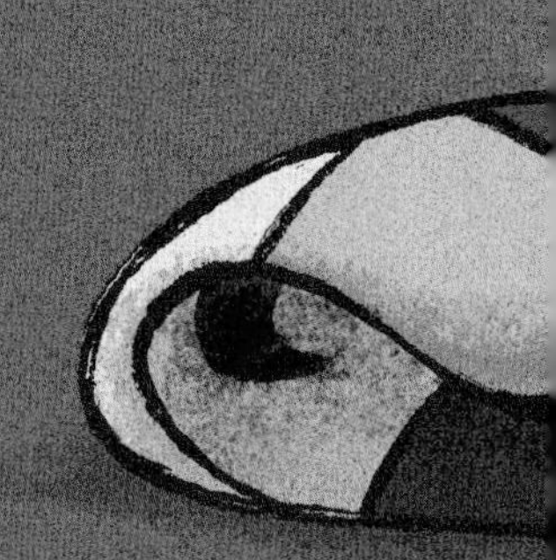

What do **MONSTERS**
snuggle with?

MONSTERS
snuggle with
TUBAS!

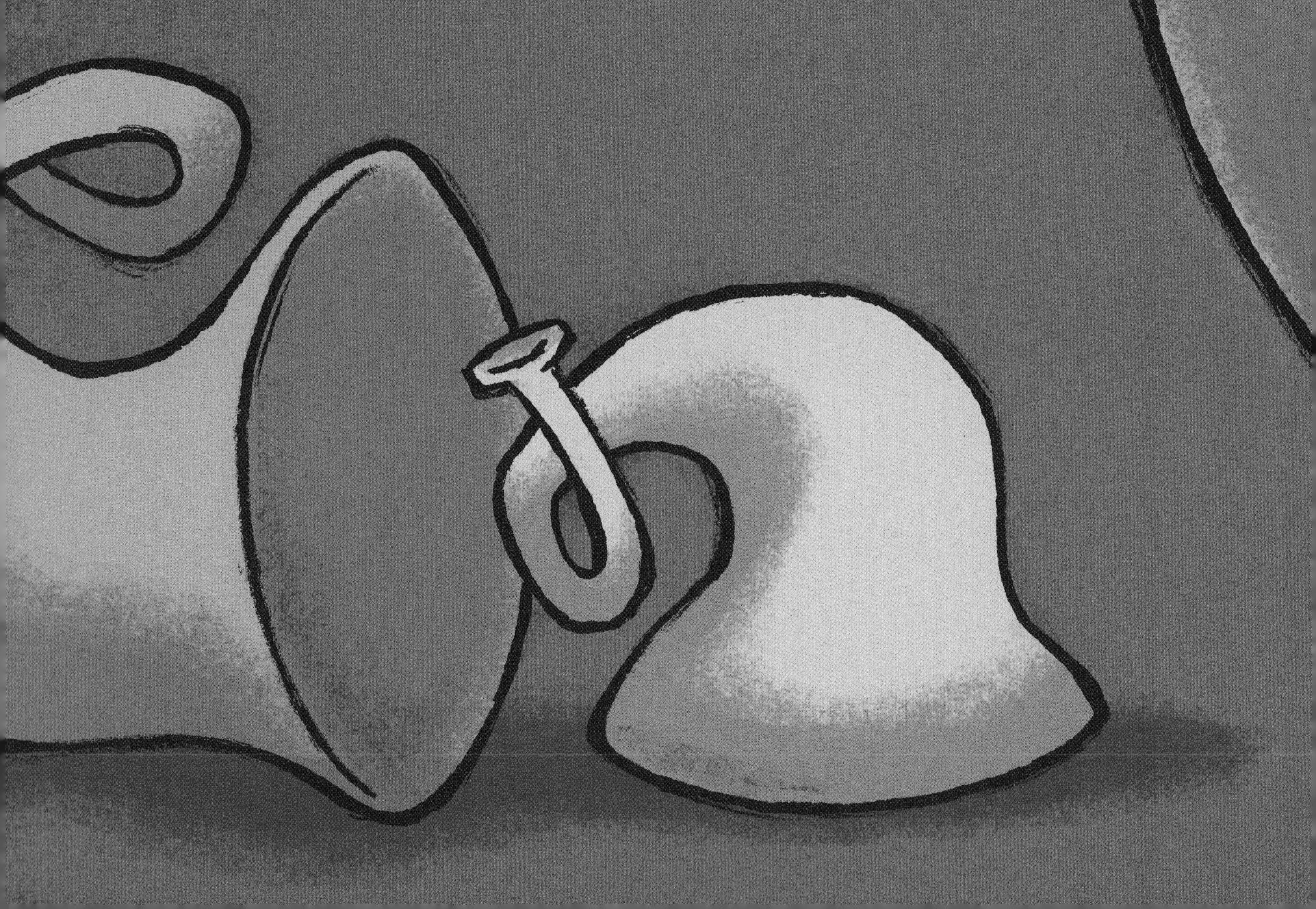

MONSTERS
clean their teeth.

How do **MONSTERS**
clean their teeth?

MONSTERS
clean their
teeth with an
OCTOPUS!

MONSTERS
need to go potty.

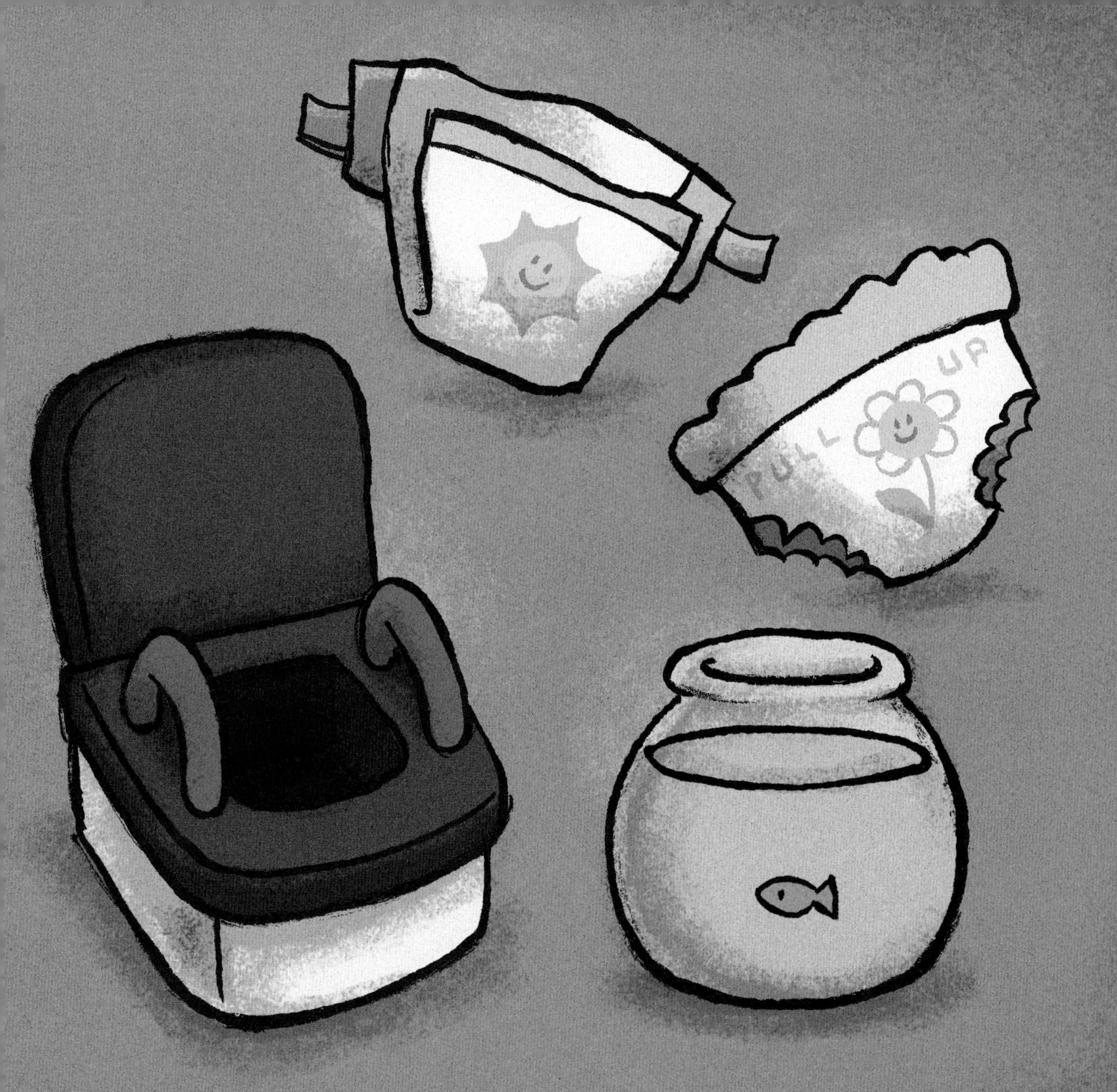

Where do **MONSTERS** go?

MONSTERS
go in the
TOILET!

(Whew! It's a good thing
MONSTERS know where to go.)

MONSTERS love
night-night kisses.

Whom do **MONSTERS** love to kiss?

Night-
night,
Mommy.

Night-
night,
Daddy.

Night-night, Baby.

And night-night, **PIZZA!**